POW!

A PEANUTS™ Collection

CHARLES M. SCHULZ

Andrews McMeel Publishing®

a division of Andrews McMeel Universal

41

46

49

58

82

84

108

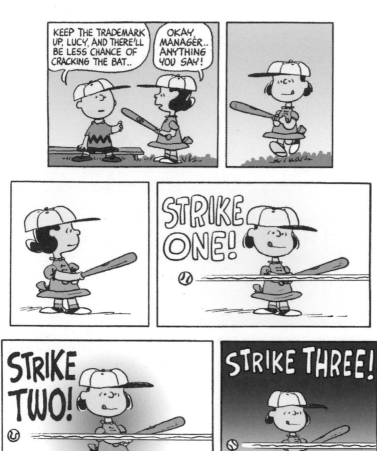

ALL RIGHT! EVERYBODY OVER HERE ON THE DOUBLE! LET'S GO!

OKAY, TEAM, THIS IS THE START OF A NEW SEASON, AND I HAVE A FEW WORDS TO SAY..

NOW, I THINK NO ONE WILL DENY THAT SPIRIT PLAYS AN IMPORTANT ROLE IN WINNING BALL GAMES

SOME MIGHT SAY THAT IT PLAYS THE MOST IMPORTANT ROLE..

THE DESIRE TO WIN IS WHAT MAKES A TEAM GREAT..WINNING IS EVERYTHING!

THE ONLY THING THAT MATTERS IS TO COME IN FIRST PLACE!

WHAT I'M TRYING TO SAY IS THAT NO ONE EVER REMEMBERS WHO COMES IN SECOND PLACE!

I DO, CHARLIE BROWN...IN 1928, THE GIANTS AND PHILADELPHIA FINISHED SECOND..IN 1929, IT WAS PITTSBURGH AND THE YANKEES..IN 1930, IT WAS CHICAGO AND WASHINGTON..IN 1931, IT WAS THE GIANTS AND THE YANKEES..IN 1932, IT WAS PITTSBURGH AND...

AND ANOTHER GREAT SEASON GETS UNDERWAY!

SCHULZ

147

THIS GUY SAYS FOR ME TO TELL YOU THAT IF YOU THROW ANYTHING THAT EVEN **LOOKS** LIKE IT MIGHT BE A BEAN-BALL, HE'S GOING TO COME OUT HERE AND POUND YOU RIGHT INTO THE GROUND!

THAT'S THE WAY JOSÉ PETERSON HIT THE YEAR HIS FAMILY LIVED IN NEW MEXICO...

.640

THAT'S THE WAY JOSÉ PETERSON HIT THE YEAR HIS FAMILY LIVED IN NORTH DAKOTA...

.850

NOW, LOOK, CHUCK... HERE'S THE WAY YOUR NEW LINEUP CAN GO...

WITH JOSÉ PETERSON AT SECOND AND ME TAKING OVER THE MOUND CHORES, YOU'RE GOING TO HAVE A GREAT TEAM, YES, SIR!

NOBODY WILL BE ABLE TO BEAT US! WHY, YOU'LL PROBABLY BE SELECTED "MANAGER OF THE YEAR"!

FOR WHAT?

180

202

205

CHARLIE BROWN'S All★Stars

MORE TO EXPLORE!

In addition to all these great *Peanuts* cartoons, here are some cool activities and fun facts for you related to baseball and comic strips. Thanks to our friends at the Charles M. Schulz Museum and Research Center in Santa Rosa, California, for helping us out with these.

Learn the Different Positions in Baseball

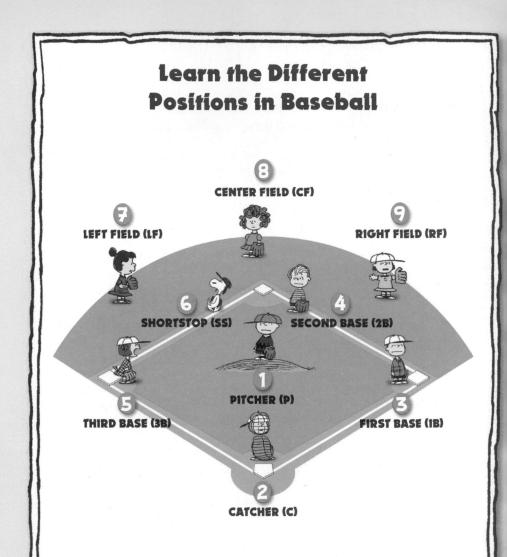

The All-Stars' Roster

P: Charlie Brown   **2B:** Linus   **LF:** Violet

C: Schroeder   **3B:** Patty   **CF:** Frieda

1B: Shermy   **SS:** Snoopy   **RF:** Lucy

Baseball Positions

There are nine positions in baseball. The number assigned to each position is used to record fielding plays on the scorecard.

1 PITCHER: The pitcher throws the ball to the catcher over the plate, trying to make the ball hard for the batter to hit. While it's good for a pitcher to be able to throw fast pitches, it's more important for a pitcher to have control. Control means he should be able to throw strikes, using different pitches.

2 CATCHER: The catcher stands/squats behind home plate and catches the ball when the batter misses or doesn't swing. The catcher is like the quarterback of the team, since he can see the whole field from his position. The catcher calls the pitches for the pitcher, keeps track of balls and strikes, and reminds the other players about them.

3 FIRST BASE: The first baseman protects and plays near first base. Since this position is involved in many plays, it's important that he catches the ball well. It's also helpful if he is tall and left-handed.

4 SECOND BASE: This position protects second base and the gaps on either side of the base, working closely with the shortstop.

5 THIRD BASE: The third baseman protects and plays near third base. She usually gets the least action of any of the infielders, but her defense is critical on preventing scoring.

6 SHORTSTOP: The shortstop is the most important defensive player on the team, usually positioned in the gap between second and third base. He needs to be able to field and throw well.

7 LEFT FIELDER: The left fielder needs to have good fielding and catching skills and is responsible for backing up third base.

8 CENTER FIELDER: The center fielder covers the most ground of the outfielders and needs to be able to move fast and throw far. She backs up second base.

9 RIGHT FIELDER: The right fielder's most important role is to back up first base as there is so much action at that position.

Make Your Own Pennant

MATERIALS: construction paper; pencil; ruler; scissors; tape; straw; pre-printed alphabet letters; stickers; crayons, and/or markers

INSTRUCTIONS:

1 Use the pencil and ruler to mark the outline of the pennant, using this shape as a guide.

2 Cut out the pennant.

3 Tear a piece of tape, place it along the flat edge of the triangle, and then around one end of the straw.

4 Decorate with the letters, stickers, crayons, and/or markers.

ALL-STARS

Take Me Out to the Ballpark Field Mix

INGREDIENTS:

- 1 cup pretzel sticks (like bats!)
- 1 cup mini marshmallows (like baseballs!)
- 1 cup toasted wheat cereal (like bases!)
- 1 cup peanuts (because it's baseball!)

INSTRUCTIONS:

Mix each ingredient in a large, airtight plastic container and shake. Then share with your friends!

Charles M. Schulz and
Peanuts Fun Facts

🖐 Charles Schulz drew 17,897 comic strips throughout his career.

🖐 Schulz was first published in Ripley's newspaper feature *Believe It or Not* in 1937. He was fifteen years old and the drawing was of the family dog.

🖐 From birth, comics played a large role in Schulz's life. At just two days old, an uncle nicknamed Schulz "Sparky" after the horse Spark Plug from the *Barney Google* comic strip. And that's what he was called for the rest of his life.

🖐 In a bit of foreshadowing, Schulz's kindergarten teacher told him, "Someday, Charles, you're going to be an artist."

🖐 Growing up, Schulz had a black-and-white dog that later became the inspiration for Snoopy—the same dog that Schulz drew for Ripley's *Believe It or Not*. The dog's name was Spike.

🖐 Charles Schulz earned a star on the Hollywood Walk of Fame in 1996.

Learn How Comics Can Reflect Life

MATERIALS: blank piece of paper, pencil, markers or colored pencils

1. Make seven blank cartoon panels.

2. Look at the example across the page to see how Charles Schulz used his own life in his strips—even painful experiences like losing a baseball game—and turned them into strips. Think of something that has happened to you at home or school that had a big impact on you.

3. Once you have decided on a story you want to tell, draw it in seven panels. Remember, it should have a beginning, a middle, and an end.

4. In the first panel, give your comic strip a name.

An example from Schulz's life:

"Charlie Brown's ill-fated baseball games mirror some of Schulz's childhood games. Schulz's team did in fact, once lose a baseball game by a score of 40 to 0. The March 23, 1952, strip (shown opposite) is the first *Peanuts* Sunday strip to feature the all-American sport."

—from *Celebrating Peanuts: 60 Years*, Andrews McMeel Publishing, 2009.

About the Charles M. Schulz Museum

The Schulz Museum and Research Center officially opened August 17, 2002, when a dream became a reality. For many years, thousands of admirers flocked to see Charles M. Schulz's original comic strips at exhibitions outside of Santa Rosa because his work didn't have a proper home. As the fiftieth anniversary of *Peanuts* drew closer, the idea that there ought to be a museum to hold all Schulz's precious work began to grow. Schulz didn't think of himself as a "museum piece" and was, therefore, understandably reluctant about accepting the idea. That left the "vision" work to local cartoon historian Mark Cohen, wife Jeannie Schulz, and longtime friend Edwin Anderson. Schulz's enthusiasm for the museum was kindled in 1997 after seeing the inspired and playful creations by artist and designer Yoshiteru Otani for the Snoopy Town shops in Japan. From that point plans for the museum moved steadily along. A board of directors was established, a mission statement adopted, and the architect and contractor were hired. The location of the museum is particularly fitting—sited across the street from Snoopy's Home Ice, the ice arena and coffee shop that Schulz built in 1969, and one block away from the studio where Schulz worked and created for thirty years. Since its opening in 2002, thousands of visitors from throughout the world have come to the museum to see the enduring work of Charles M. Schulz which will be enjoyed for generations to come.

Even More to Explore!

These additional sources will be helpful if you wish to learn more about Charles Schulz, the Charles M. Schulz Museum and Research Center, *Peanuts*, or the art of cartooning.

WEBSITES:

www.schulzmuseum.org
- Official website of the Charles M. Schulz Museum and Research Center.

www.peanuts.com
- Thirty days' worth of *Peanuts* strips. Character profiles. Timeline about the strip. Character print-outs for coloring. Info on fellow cartoonists' tributes to Charles Schulz after he passed away.

www.fivecentsplease.com
- Recent news articles and press releases on Charles Schulz and *Peanuts*. Links to other *Peanuts*-themed websites. Info on *Peanuts* products.

www.toonopedia.com
- Info on *Peanuts* and many, many other comics—it's an "encyclopedia of 'toons."

www.gocomics.com
- Access to popular and lesser-known comic strips, as well as editorial cartoons.

www.reuben.org
- Official website of the National Cartoonists Society. Info on how to become a professional cartoonist. Info on awards given for cartooning.

www.kingfeatures.com and www.amuniversal.com
- Newspaper syndicate websites. Learn more about the distribution of comics to newspapers.

Andrews McMeel Publishing
a division of Andrews McMeel Universal
1130 Walnut Street, Kansas City, Missouri 64106

www.andrewsmcmeel.com

www.peanuts.com

16 17 18 19 20 SDB 10 9 8 7 6 5 4 3

ISBN: 978-1-4494-5826-3

Library of Congress Control Number: 2014931549

Made by:
Shenzhen Donnelley Printing Company Ltd.
Address and location of manufacturer:
No. 47, Wuhe Nan Road, Bantian Ind. Zone,
Shenzhen China, 518129
3rd Printing—3/21/16

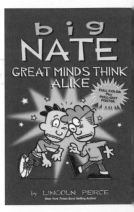
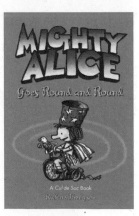
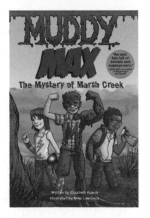
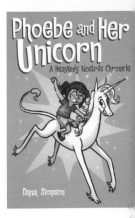